NINETEEN STORIES

JOSEPH VOELBEL

To
My Father

"At times some birds, a horse,
have saved the ruins of an amphitheater."
– Jorge Luis Borges

CONTENTS

NINETEEN STORIES

(Inside the Mind of) Le Comte

I'd only met Le Comte once. It was in London, circa 1825. I was a child, a queer boy of eight, with uneven legs which caused me to walk at a hobble. I remember in peculiar detail the strange brightness of the sun that day, and waiting expectantly to meet him, also the manner in which he tapped his cane to the ground as he'd exited his carriage, and the tone of voice of my mother, a timbre I'd never heard before or since. We visited the rose garden and picnicked there. They seemed to understand each other intimately, but on opposing sides of an issue. They spent most of that afternoon quibbling; I remember my stomach going soft and being unable to finish my food. My Uncle had said, 'You've got to eat my boy, in spite of all the hullaballoo!' And then he laughed like a lion.

That was the only time Le Comte entered my life, so as to just why he'd left me with the most intimate details of his mind was beyond me. My mother thought it might be because I was a cripple, and that he pitied me or the fact that I'd studied at Oxford, which meant I wasn't a total dope. But then she added more certainly that it was most likely due to the simple truth that he didn't trust anybody else in the family.

I spent a great deal of last year at his summer estate. I would arrive in the morning by carriage, have a cup of tea and open at random one of the hundreds of dusty journals. They occupied the study like learned poltergeists, perching, hanging, veering. They were of the most ornate appearance. Not only were they firmly bound, and self-published, but they were composed in illuminated script. If my brief stint in graphology taught me anything, it was that Le Comte's penmanship was fascinatingly deft, and his swooping j's and well proportioned w's were trademarks of both ostentatiousness and temperance. To find both in a single stroke of the pen was rare.

At first I didn't read them, I couldn't, they were too alien. I will explain this otherness shortly. Instead, I held them. I picked them up and set them down. I ran my forefinger along their spines and turned their pages. This was what my late uncle would have referred to as a metaphysical exercise in psychometry.

Because I couldn't actually extract a single notion of what any of the journals meant I considered discontinuing the project altogether. It wasn't until I threw one on the ground out of frustration and it landed in front of the study's mirror that I realized portions of the composition had been done in reverse. This would have been a relatively easy thing to spot initially, but was made unidentifiable because sentences had also been written upside down and in hybrids of Greek, French, Arabic, Italian, Chinese, Sumerian cuneiform, Egyptian hieroglyphs and another unidentifiable language (consisting of variegated patterns of dots and wavy lines). Upon closer inspection I discovered even single words were in some cases, portmanteaus of these languages. It was an etymological poetry, of sorts. Each sentence, since written backwards and inverted, would only be clear when turned over and seen through the looking glass. In order for the next word to be what followed the previous, I had to start reading at the end of the journal and go from right to left and bottom to top until I got to the beginning of the journal, which was its natural end.

By way of this process three journals proved modestly revealing, and from them I managed to cobble together strands of coherence, a semblance of what may have been intended amidst all the pages of all the journals. What I gathered from the first journal were two items of note: a spat of Arabic poetry that described the universe as we know it, and a Chinese description of the phenomenon of moving objects with your mind. The first was composed in the vein of Sufic poetry and it read, roughly translated, *the inhalation of / God*, the second was the Chinese character for wind beside the character for hand, which roughly translated meant, hand of the wind, or more precisely, hand on the wind.

The second journal remained impenetrable. Filled primarily with that otherly langauge consisting of differently spaced dots and multi-directed wavy lines, the only discernible characters were sporadic hieroglyphs mixed with cuneiform. I wrote out a few of those otherly characters from the second journal, if only to feel an alien set of letters upon my hand. There was one extractible datum from the second journal. An inscription written upon the base of its frontispiece, which read: *Hic eſt draco caudam ſuam devorans*, which was Latin for 'the dragon devours his tail'. It was below a picture of the same, set in front of a collapsed wall, and a dirt road, in some quaint middle-age village.

The third journal I was able to have some success with as bits of it had been composed in English. It consisted primarily of a collection of vague alchemical aphorisms, for example, "the androgen seeks fire by reunification" and philosophical axioms such as, "every action is accounted for, every thought an action". Romantic epithets also peppered its pages, "give not that which you do not have to give, lest you lose yourself", contrarily followed by, "give of thyself, until there is nothing more". Most of this seemed trivial, if perhaps arcane, and yet all of which, apparently moved its author to some degree.

Despite these kernels of extraction, the only part I really understood clearly in the third journal was a quote by a philosopher I'd never heard of and amidst all my scholarly research, declare does not exist, a man named Ludwig Wittgenstein, from a book called, *Tractatus Logico-Philosophicus*, which employed seven groups of aphorisms. The seventh of which was a single line, most memorable and instructive, which was, "*Wovon man nicht sprechen kann, daruber muss man schweigen.*" (Whereof one cannot speak, thereof one must be silent). From there I endeavored to go no further.

Harold

Harold often suspected he heard a low pitch humming. After a number of months he figured out it was just the sound of the laundry machine next-door. At present the street light outside his apartment window hurt his temples, and caused him to squint at the object of his study.

Harold stood up from his chair and stuck his hands in his jean pockets, looked about his apartment, and smiled. He enjoyed doing things that were audaciously normal, like sticking one's hands in one's pockets. Harold often acted "normal" *on purpose*, for if he behaved how he wished to behave, he gathered that society might not be able to grip him, and then he could become unstuck, which *was* a slippery slope. Not for Harold but for people who weren't proficient at sliding. There was no question Harold still possessed all his marbles; the question pertaining to what he'd been squinting at was related to society's apperception of those marbles. Playing marbles as a child had been interesting to him, a place between aesthetics and physics, bookended by his thumb and index finger.

The street lights that caused him to squint, the volume of intercoms on airplanes, and a good many other things, Harold felt to be askew. That included but wasn't limited to, stores beeping upon our arrival, the way pop songs carried a similar amorphous tune and radio announcers that nondescript drawl - even across languages, how people said, "fine," when feeling morose and spoke somberly even when there wasn't much to complain about, and how people assume what they have *read* must be *true*. Oh, and not to mention the inexhaustible societal desire to relate, often again and again, stories of encounters with celebrity, no doubt spurred on by some warped conception of deity and magazines that rubbed off on your fingers. For these and other reasons, when it came to worldviews, Harold preferred the scenic route. If worldviews were planets Harold felt he'd be Pluto, as he spent much of his time on the periphery of our ideological orbit, and with such feathery mass that other planets began to accuse him of not existing. This evening, just what Harold was squinting at was the story in question.

Earlier that day, Harold had been on his bicycle, where he spun his wheels towards his destiny. He rode along a row of pines, and halfway between noon and dusk, he stopped, to sit among the fallen needles and beneath the tall trees, for a meditation. The scent of pine transported him to when he used to follow with bare feet the path of the deer, discover porcupine quills, and raise them high in the air like Excalibur.

The difference between that memory and that moment earlier today had become indistinguishable for Harold. This was an instance of sliding and it hinged on settling into this feeling of indistinguishability. From this Prosperoic center, a deep still well formed, and within it Harold pursued an expansion of his chest cavity – his rib cage broadened like the bellows of an ancient accordion. Just then, breath and spirit married, and were both within and about him.

Harold knew he knew that much about that but not that much about what he'd been squinting at.

Just what Harold was squinting at was a drawing of a dream he'd dreamed. Upon closer inspection he realized that if he could dream any dream again he'd dream *this* dream, again. For this dream was slipping into his reality like the yolk of a punctured egg gliding across the plate of his consciousness. The space between what he dreamed and how things seemed was diminishing. To Harold, this particular dream arrived like a large ship coming into the harbor. He could see it from shore, and waited for it expectantly. He just was not sure how it was going to dock.

Harold hoped the guidance of the lighthouse would keep it off the rocks, and he prayed that the mighty tides of Neptune would carry it across the vast expanse, and onto the dock of his life. Though still ashore, Harold in this instance, realized he was also the captain, but that this captain was the truest version of himself, navigating from yonder to burst back into his reality, that is, to come ashore and meet Harold. While squinting Harold could barely make out the picture in front of him, of himself in this dream, squinting to see the ship off in the distance, jumping up and down on the sand and waiving his arms in the air like he'd held those porcupine quills as a child.

At present, he was only half-there; he'd stepped one leg into this vision to replay the previous evening's journey and its meaning with respect to the apotheosis of his soul.

These thoughts hung about his head as if his skull were partially submerged under water, but upended, as the water was above him, and he below it. This *supermerging* occurred for Harold at his own discretion, and as his cogitations swashed about in this mercurial elixir, mixed partly from memory and partly by imagination, he realized that in these instances, when he squinted because the light was too bright, he felt that whatever he could hope to say about his dream with words would be *at least* the distance his feet were from how far his eyes could see.

The Pilgrim

The Pilgrim walked on his path in short resolute paces. A wind swept in from the west bringing specks of leaves with it that formed little eddies around his ankles. Though it was still a several day journey eastward, his forehead remained fixed on the mountainous peak. He eyed that celestial ball of fire hovering in the sky, which slowly descended upon the mountain's silhouette, gilding it with that golden cloak which glimmered during this royal passage of day.

A small sack cloth slung over his shoulder bounced against his spine as he walked. It contained three uncut pieces of quartz crystal, an anachronistic post script from an Argentinian author pertaining to the first use of a parenthetical, and a polaroid of his Father in front of an all-white Buick in a 1970's midwestern American suburb.

The Pilgrim lie on his side. Ashes fell upon his face from the kindle fire consisting of twigs and dried bark, which burned low upon the ground. An old lady with a donkey hitched to a wagon passed by. The churning of the wagon's wheels creaked out into the night like the moans of some antique mechanical mammal. As his eyelids closed, amidst this veil of night, The Pilgrim's thoughts journeyed into what became an elongated tunnel. The end of which contained a reoccurring vision he'd had since childhood of an inside-out firefly, flapping its red, orange and yellow wings, on a blindingly white day, above a crisp green lawn.

The sun rose and fell three times while this vision remained fixed firmly within him.

That next morning The Pilgrim reached the foot of the mountain, where a spring fed pool awaited. The Pilgrim thought, "these waters are fresh from the veins of Mother and carry its vitality and constitution. I will wash myself here in a ritualistic fashion." He placed his palms in the prayer position and closed his eyes, then disrobed, waded into the water and slowly let the oxygen out of his lungs until he'd immersed himself entirely. The pressure of his knees tucked into his chest, and his gut spiraling into a ball of steel, allowed for warmth in his core at the bottom of this cool mountain fed spring. Once there, he wondered not and knew not. Not but the image of a fire-fly, that polar star of his spiritual aspirations, fixed in an ever-North.

The Pilgrim began his ascent as if he'd never lost sight of it. He'd first seen it as a ten year old boy, after his teacher passed him a note, written in all caps with red felt tip pen (at a modest height and equidistant spacing) upon the inside cover of a book that contained portraits of all his classmates. It read, "Aim for the stars," the Young Pilgrim looked up with suns in his eyes, right then, and for the first time, he saw wings flapping all around him.

The Pilgrim seemed to travel faster than his surroundings, they whisked passed him on the path like the frames of reality viewed from moving trains, as if he were the film, and different parts of himself lit up as they slid through the window.

The Pilgrim placed his head to the ground at the mouth of the cave. Entering slowly he sat in front of a kind being with a warm face and a soft glow, who began pouring him a cup of tea.

"You may ask three questions. But first, have some tea and let us drink in one another."

"Yes, of course. Thank you."

They drank their tea on a cloud of silence. At length, the Pilgrim spoke, "Pray tell, wise one, what can you teach me of God?" The radiant being took a small sip and presented an amicable smile,

"Keep God on your lips, for holy words are like a honey that attract the ears of those who listen for sweetness."

"Yes, of course. Pray tell, wise one, what can you teach me of Spirit?"

"Always accept an offering of water, for this is Spirit in form, and it is being given unto you."

"Yes, of course. Pray tell, wise one, what can you teach me of myself?"

Light caught the surface of The Pilgrim's tea and it shimmered, "A new star appears in the night's sky each time someone awakens."

"Am I awakened?"

"Three questions, Young Pilgrim."

The Pilgrim bowed, and rose silently. As he backed away, the wise one's voice entered his mind, but in the timbre of that elementary school teacher, and at the decibel of a whisper.

"Stars are God's fireflies."

Carried by this thought, The Pilgrim passed beyond the threshold of the cave.

The Structure

The Structure was erected so as to be vacated. Every brick, slab of mortar and bead of sweat invested in its creation was built on the premise that its occupants would one day be none. Indeed, the intent of The Structure, its very essence, was to house nothing. This premise struck most as absurd. Why make something with the hope it shouldn't exist? However, the builders believed that, with respect to this structure, no longer needing to fulfill its function was the function it was designed to fulfill. The Structure facilitated this progression from needing, to not needing itself.

Long foreseen was the impermanence of the structure. Such an outcome was implicit in its birthing, inherent to its character. The origins of The Structure were transcendent and non-linear.

The development from these origins remains shrouded in an unknowing, unknowing as a characteristic of untold impact. Its fruits were of items materializing, names changing, liquids turned to stone.

Early versions of The Structure were austere, mere wooden benches and fire pits. Later iterations tallied centuries of craft and wielded colors of exquisite magnitude that captivated and awed its occupants, depicting eras of mythos – ancient symbols pressed upon glass, chipped out of marble and rolled up into incense.

Throughout its years, a curious and yearning type found their way inside its doors. Some were attracted by the craftsmanship. Others, the location itself. They showed up with problems, offering slightly ajar doors into themselves, looking to fit in, to commune. They listened. They prayed. They sang. They became penitent. All of which served as a figurative as well as metaphysical declaration of the function of The Structure, to create sanctity within its occupants.

Details surrounding the collapse of The Structure remain a matter of speculation.

The Author

The Author preferred to write by the light of a candle and from the form of his own pen after the sky turned pink with indecision. His work carried well past the hour of the wolf, when things became dark and bone cold, and the night turned ambivalent to the existence of sleeping vessels.

One eve, whilst the moon waxed along its parabolic course in the sky, The Author found his work had taken on the uncharacteristic nakedness of first person. Now, he was not composing, but instead, investigating his own unending capacity for introspection. It was as if a dark city had been pulled over his eyes, and there was no other recourse than to shine a light to see where he was coming from. He had the sneaking suspicion that he was not alone. Yet, the nature of the company also felt like an extension of himself.

Occasionally, amidst an array of seemingly innocuous activities, this sensation arrived within him. It inspired a sense of catching up to what he'd frequently thought he might become, and at other times, a sense of being behind what he hoped he would become. In a sense this sensation was always distant from him, like the ever folding paradox of Zeno, or perhaps as the countryside appears from the eyes of a hawk traveling this way and that along its peripatetic course, and yet it provided him a deep exhilaration.

For it seemed, as of late, that The Author had entered a corridor that ran parallel to his life, a hallway lined with glass walls; on the other side of the glass, his usual life as he had known it; the person in the corridor, one who is interested in this life that he is living. At moments like these, it was as if he'd stepped into his own observation, albeit unknowingly, and only for a brief instant, and because of this, became an unwitting observer of his own observation of himself.

This sense of an observer in his life began after he'd undergone, what western psychologists would refer to as a peak experience, and eastern adepts a mystical experience. This particular experience transpired after extensive contemplation of an illuminated script and was part of the unforeseeable consequences involved in such heavy metaphysical lifting.

Throughout his life these sensations occurred as eidetically as any prophetic vision. They happened in quivers, contained a not-there-ness, like the mutual presence and absence of a harmonic tone. Whereas, The Author used to fear there was someone behind the glass, looking, now he felt the heartbeat of the one who observed him.

Sander

As a child Sander followed the ascent of balloons until it hurt to look anymore. While he walked down the sidewalk streetlights clipped out as if on switches. His impassioned comments were periodically accompanied by an unrelated noise in the room, be it the unintentional bang of an elbow on a table, a window rattled by the wind in its frame, or the sudden and unprompted whirr of a mechanical instrument. It was as if, on occasion, when keyed up, he spoke in a physical sense, or more properly stated, what he said, *mattered*.

When people asked him who he was he responded through his eyes. Those eyes became lighthouses for ships at sea. The houses that marked the water from the land and prevented everything from blurring and turning to blue.

Sander regularly conversed with angels and other celestial folk. Late in life, after perusing Emmanuel Swedenborg's auto-biographical tale, *Life on Other Planets*, he deemed these incidents credible. The Swedish mystic's experience with angels were well documented, and amused him. Like Swedenborg, Sander rarely found himself alone when at work. Angels gathered around him in crowds, in the evenings, during his compositions.

Curious creatures, angels. They were quite bothered by human's ears being so stopped up. Otherwise, they were downright jovial. They began arriving shortly after Sander's mother contracted cancer. She'd seen a white light. She told Sander that the brightness of that light revealed the distance she was from God. "And it was so bright." She'd gasped.

That night as Sander fell asleep, he experienced, for the first time, a crack in his life, where the light flooded in. It contained both an earthly warmth and a celestial hue. After that, peeks between worlds became more frequent. They appeared on puddles, echoed in door frames, and whistled amidst will-o'-wisps. His pupils would widen.

When things got to be too much Sander tucked his legs together and retreated to the sensation of a waterfall rising up his spine. This caused his eye to shine in a radiant astral light. His *chakra* (that 'wheel' about the human forehead), became anointed, for someone put oil there, and he received this *Christ*ening. Biblical scholars speculate this *ajna* is what Jesus was referring to in Matthew 6:22, when he said: "The light of the body is the eye: if therefore thine eye be single, thy whole body shall be full of light."

Sander's spiritual sight rested above his regular eyes, the eyes that perceived the ordinary world of common everyday experience. Religions acknowledged this taller point of view in their headware. As Sander's eye became unclouded, he quivered.

The angels heard this resonance as it reverberated off the walls of the heavenly realms, and performed a calibration which constituted itself as a murmur in the gut of his longing, a soft urging, which sounded to them like a mob of whales swimming, or parade of elephants running.

That next morning Sander's eye burned bright like a lantern in the heart of darkness. Reality teethed. Moments dissolved and expanded. Maya swept away like a gail upon desert sands effacing the ancient visage of Ozymandius. Golden scales rang out within his ears.

The fulcrum of existence seemed to float in a space only discernible on the foggy face of a mirror made from an exhalation blown closely upon it, as if it were all no more than a plume of steam upon a sleek surface, where one could write a name with their finger, or wipe clean with the sweep of a palm.

As he no longer sought to hide, Sander's wings became unclipped. There was nothing left to do but see and see he did.

"Maybe that's why all plants," he thought, "like humans, turn their heads to face the sun."

A Hagiographic Account of
Sebastian Featherwood Delvantino

Sebastian Featherwood Delvantino was a prominent thirteenth century Italian mystic and polymath, christened to sainthood in the 15th century under Pope Gregory XII following a rapid succession of events which proved veridical a series of glossolalic prognostications made nearly two centuries prior by the mystic himself. In his time, the Italian people lauded Delvantino for his adept engineering of Le Monte Arch, the eastern most entrance of Pisa's boundaries, as well as several sacred burial chambers, and not the least for his academic assistance to Leonardo Bonacci, who is responsible for introducing the now commonplace numbers one through nine.

The numbers were presented by Bonacci, with the aid of Delvantino, and his expertise in ancient calculation systems, in the book *Liber Abaci*, which established the metrological superiority of its Arabic and Hindu mathematical origins. Delvantino worked alongside Bonacci to uncover what is now known as the Fibonacci sequence (Phi + Bonacci), its metrical processes and sequencing being derived from the prosody of the Vedas, a subject Delvantino enlightened Bonacci on during the course of his research; unfortunately, Sebastian Featherwood Delvatino's sacerdotal initiation appointed by Pope Gregory XII was redacted in the 17th century under the reign of Pope Leo XI, for reasons at present unknown, wherefrom he faded into relative obscurity.

The Examination

The Examination was administered without regard to the participant. Those who knew they'd been examined had not passed. Those that had passed did not know. To ensure a continuation of results circumstances of every examination were irreproducible. Inimitability was intrinsic in examinations, due to the fact that no examination could be dictated by the constraints of space or time. This was most likely because examiners existed in neither while examinees persisted in both.

Thousands of exams were held daily. To ensure a passing score examinees vowed acceptance in the face of the inexplicable. The degree of unlikeliness present in any given circumstance, as well as how uncertain one was what was being observed is real, gave reasonable indication as to the likelihood of an examination being administered. One examinee, simply as a preparatory exercise, wrote a facsimile of Proust's *In Search of Lost Time*, without lifting his pen. Another success transpired in a handshake. An infamous failure involved composing a millennium of weather patterns into song. Potential examinees found themselves in foreign countries, forging new patterns of speech, manners of living, and diet. Others assumed new bodies, of animals even. Still more endured severe losses of prestige, faith, or family, became divested of fortunes or were bequeathed maps with no X.

The regimens proscribed for each examinee were unascertainable by anyone other than oneself. Furthermore, said understanding could not be explained to anyone, or by anyone, particularly to oneself *if* they understood it.

Curious attributes of examinees abound. With an eye for these things such aspects can be spotted. Symptoms include the ability to perceive thought without speech, the unintended arrival of companions, and dreaming in groups. Some have been said to even have the capacity to not die, or to pretend to, appearing upon riversides, in mountain caves, or outside Spanish mercados, as necessary...

Long safeguarded are the answers to The Examination. It has been alleged there is a singular key, and that that key may in fact be a single word with a potency not dissimilar to that of the Tetragrammaton, (a four letter name for God that cannot be spoken) and if known, although each examination is inherently unknown, and when spoken, (what exactly may constitute speech remains debated), behaved like a skeleton key to every other examination.

Pursuit for this key was long been underway. Information as to its exact nature trades at a price similar to a bundle of small countries. Anyone who thinks they can purchase this key would not understand what The Examination is for, or how to take it.

It has also been whispered in dark rooms that The Examination is a hoax, or that it is autobiographic, and its proctors are simply future versions of ourselves.

The Watchers

Most had disappeared. The few who remained on earth lived in relative obscurity. Their number had originally been two hundred. It is said that when they descended from the fifth heaven, and looked upon the women of the earth, that they yearned for them, and lay with them. Those children became known as men of great renown.

The Watchers taught the people of the earth many things, both spiritual and physical, that well exceeded anything proto-human had cobbled together up until that point. In essence the Watchers provided a pedagogical roadmap to the great order of the universe, and its laws and characteristics in relation to man. The people across the continents of the earth learned for the first time: the cycles of the moon and secrets of the sun, the position of the earth as relevant to the stars, the energetic meridians written upon their own bodies, and how to stimulate them; the diverse applications of various combinations of herbs, and the sacred placement of monuments upon intersecting leigh-lines in the earth's body. In short, the construction of cities and cultures.

The Watchers also taught protohuman how to prophesy, the art of divination and its variegated methods, fortunes from the patterns of flight among flocks of birds, the casting of lots, the tossing of runes, the spread of tea-leaves in the bottom of a cup. They also learned the types of dreams that come true, the difference between arid and moist soil and the art of metallurgy. Thus, protohuman deemed The Watchers, "Gods", and worshipped them as bringers of knowledge, and workers of high magic.

As many Gods covered the land, protohumans applied their mastery over metal to make swords, bayonets, arrow tips, and other pointed objects, and pointed them at one another, declaring their God to be the most worthy God. The protohumans hadn't known such power since before the fall, and they knew not how to wield it, and so they lashed out upon one another's beliefs.

Although The Watchers brought vast knowledge to the place under the Kingdom of Heaven, due to their breeding with protohuman, and teaching of the secret trades, God decreed that The Watchers would perish during the deluge, alongside the humans whom wouldn't desist in the heightening of their tower.

The flood signaled a fresh start on all fronts. The Watchers were forgiven for their unauthorized distribution of divine powers and humanity was pardoned for its engagement with them. A redistribution of roles in the heavens and on earth occurred, and man began again, anew. Some honors and privileges were reinstated.

Certain arrogant Watchers survived the great flood. Afraid of their death, they hid away from judgement in the inner caverns of earth. These Watchers resurfaced to assist false prophets whom still aimed to control human kind. These Watchers owned much of the earth, and sought sovereignty over all whom dwelt upon it. They planned against God and fled in the presence of his emissaries.

Their wicked intentions still served a divine role in the metamorphosis for the very part of humanity that has sought to deter the spiritual evolution of the planetary body, by the force of its deterrence, has increased the power necessary to overcome it.

Whereupon bursts the radiance of Love, makes absent the presence of its absence.

Tabernus Adepti

The Lodge of the Adepts, or *Tabernus Adepti,* is an astral order of divine initiates from different races, creeds and continents throughout time immemorial. The order has joined many lives and incarnations to assist in the awakening and unification of all beings on planet earth. Doubt not, they've infinitely vaster things to attend to, but out of compassion, selflessness, and the joy of witnessing transmutation have agreed to make the evolution of the earthly spirits a central purpose of their existence.

Many good men have spoken of it. Men of great renown. Men of anonymity. The notion that this order is hierarchical is mistaken. There are *levels* but they aren't top to bottom per se, rather more inside out. Methods of initiation remain variegated. Aptitude tests include calculation of the initiate's *proximity to heavenly awareness* in conjunction with their *desire to facilitate* the *evolution of humanity*. These are simply assessed, not judged, and whatever their degree, praised. Other applicants undergo a *willful spat of amnesia*. Some choose to remember their initiation but remain outside the *Tabernus* in service of it, charged with the duty of attracting new recruits, and nudging those whom had also purposely forgotten.

A deeper work occurs inside. The progression through this depth contains a series of inner seals, which, as opened, give rise to greater and greater degrees of self-awareness. These seals remain in place to protect us from what we are not yet prepared to see about ourselves. There is no skipping between levels because the intention to open a new level requires the completion of the previous, an alchemy in exact proportion with one's inner constitution. By engaging the faculties that develop the above mentioned skills the initiate progresses through various *seals of awareness*. Graduation from this academy means placement in a heavenly realm. Whereupon one is surrounded by what has been esoterically referred to as the *harmonice mundi*, the sound of the spheres, or quite literally, the harmonies of the world. As one might expect, such is a difficult place to venture away from.

Initiates that desire to teach and fill a more-or-less tutelary role, stay down here to help those whom have sought inwardly and begun their ascent. Other levels open with respect to each person's specialized area of study. Propositions for advancing your work into various sidereal realms of awareness, or elevated conditions of consciousness, are not a-typical.

Regardless of one's starting point in this journey, all progressions are continually moving inward, further and further, behaving something akin to the rising force inside a tornado, which forms an ascending spiralic curve, and always reaches upward to a higher mark, yet with the same angle of ascendency, until this process finally re-joins with the place where it began.

Arrival here is tantamount to a merging with the Entelech Logos, or as many great philosophers have said, like entering a circle whose center is everywhere and circumference nowhere.

The Pack

They are not angels. They are not demons. They are The Pack. Their primary imperative is protecting the corridors between dream and reality. This *is* a most complex endeavor. It involves traversing subterranean caverns, elevated chambers, and vortexual configurations. The Pack's world is one of blur, water color, and intuition. Their sensations span spectrums far beyond our capacity of sight or sound. Their daytime is illusory. Their nighttime, invisible.

As one's day is another's night, so too both waking and sleeping worlds are constantly being engaged. Since one can be awake in a dream or asleep while awake as well as the opposite, both worlds exist concurrently. Thus, spectral openings through the gates is always shifting.

The Pack knows that the veil between waking and sleeping is thinnest at dusk and dawn when the curtains between worlds become enmeshed, neither thrown open by day, nor shut tight by night. Entrance through the gates feels like being the recipient of a wink or the manner in which arrives a useful idea. Such journeys can be induced by the sudden presence or absence of rain. If you've ever met a helper, guide, or spirit ally in your dream, such a figure was most likely an emissary from The Pack.

Moving between states of waking and sleeping creates bumps in timespace, and these bumps come with a host of side effects. They may include memory loss or retrieval, time shrinking or expanding, new skills obtained and old one's lost, and especially crisp visceral sensations, flashes of insight, and spontaneous self-healing. Though these alterations are minor, and many, The Pack deems such side-effects worthwhile, in comparison to not participating in new perceptual frequencies.

The Pack monitors transitions through these gates while assisting individuals with dreamtime and day time lessons, reminding them to remain ever wakeful and thus protected.

To run, fly, or swim with The Pack is considered a high honor. Cultures practicing abilities like this include the Dogon of West Africa, whose spiritual elders, called *Hogon,* serve as guardians of their mythology, and the indigenous Aborigines of Australia, whose healers, called *Ngangkari,* act as custodians of their dreamtime memory. Let The Pack be considered synonymous with these arbiters of the great mystery, and all protectors of the portals that comprise dimensions.

The Countenance of Forgiveness

They all had a strange look on their faces. He'd been told it was human. It seemed to carry a deliberate sense of artifice like the packaging on a child's toy, protecting the illusions within. His feet moved. His fingers wiggled. His eyes carried that same strangeness he saw upon the fronts of those that slunked about and amidst the shadows of the metropolis (an odd term of endearment used by early 21st century humans to refer to what Plato allegorized in *The Republic* as The Cave). They lived in a day's dream of rest. They were the sleeping tired. He, burdened by the profound realization of selecting this journey, had only his consciousness and the solace of a breeze as his companions. Those that were close felt peculiarly distant. Many that were dead, profoundly near.

How to make something of himself when one's life was their canvas, their decisions brushstrokes in an unrelenting Garden of Forking Paths[1]. To live boldly, a fiction. To live meekly, an act of courage. He felt himself to be like the dust upon the floor of a great house, since carcassed, on some inconspicuous hillside overlooking a village which once held communion with the sky. These ideas were not his. The notion of property to him, absurd. Even in so far as we say *our*selves.

Flesh cuts smoothly as if in water. Spirit calls for peace in a temple of the profane. What is good, what is true, what is noble, encapsulated in the heights of bodies entwined, fates woven into fates, the tapestry of a comedy, a joke one's only serenity. What is evil, what is false, what is ignoble, the distance between the trough and the wave, the receding tide from the shoring of capitalism, the notion of nations, of boundaries,

---

[1] The Garden of Forking Paths (1941) by Argentinian author Jorge Luis Borges, contains the following relevant passage, "I thought of a maze of mazes, of a sinuous ever growing maze which would take in both past and future and would somehow involve the stars."

and even of names, perhaps all a perpetuation of disillusionment. He carried wisdom sheepishly, bereaved by the capacity to perceive. He sought a monk's removal. A hermit's concealment. And yet to him, these were a coward's seclusion. His defense - a sense of humor against the onslaught of animation - his only path to peace of mind. A path less traveled, a path forgotten, a path with its tracks dusted over, buried in the depths, locked into a trunk where secrets ferment, in a society of amnesiacs quoting other's false memories, feeling truth to be the letter and fact to be the word.

He, a mime, amidst a cacophony, like the impartiality of the color white within a blizzard. His dearest friends, a Rilke, a Keats, a Kafka, dead men with living ideas. Life an auction, where many spirits lie defenseless to the inculcation of commands. Buy. Sleep. Die. Repeat.

Wherefore dost your flower bloom? Of what can be said the fragrance of a flower? Paradox a precursor to that clarity that teases him. And they order coffee. And they discuss people. What is he if not they? How can he not be they? Why would he not be they? For then he is no more. If he does not perceive the piety of a vacuum, the chamber of a sound, the birth of a star, the omen of a great nation, a terrible lover, a great war, a fantastic thought, then with whom is he fighting if not himself? For those who have crest the wave, who have lifted their heads over the breakwater, who have wrought, tore, heaved and wound their way to view a partially occluded glimpse, who have stepped from the shadow and called forth their name, demanded its number be spoken, for those whom that opportunity even exists, are like prime integers - only divisible by themselves and God. (There is no limit to the number of prime numbers. There is no pattern to primes, as if they were a sort of unending imagination...)

Now they watch news. Now they take opinion as density. Now they succumb to believe the estrangement of man from the divine as the path of Reason, whom stood naked in a windowless room with a compass and a microscope. Now they are enfeebled with diminuendo, lemmings quoting medical scripture lining the well padded white pockets of doctor's coats amidst diagnostical psychoses de pharmacology, whilst kids point toy guns and say, "pow", a pattern, we split atoms.

Why? For bigger toys? To wrap bodies in plastic, artifice and dust?

An awakened age forgiven by blood let. Now there's skin in the game. Words like Matrix and Maya behave like bubble gum. You chew on them, poignantly, acceptingly, forgivingly, pursuant to the ascent, the return, the instantiation of novelty as an acceleration of gaiaic mana, wherefrom whence pendulum's cross. His words become our words. Our words become his thoughts become our thoughts becoming his words. His miracles become our miracles. He, who lined a darkened street with well lit oil lanterns, which made wide and clear the road ready for those returning, from the chasm and the ache, from the gnawing implausibility, from the headstrung reductivism...

He, who peers in store windows watching widows purchase chachkies, and thinks, what has come of the bridegrooms? Have they died in battle? Are they lost in some smokey parlor tippling beverage and chasing cards for Lady Luck's indifferent advice? Is this not also, *me*? He who wonders how to keep the gait, whilst his pockets become empty, whom demands, trumpets for his people, his culture, his planet, his family.

Those learned fools, holy fools, sacred fools, he felt them. Unknown wise-ones unknowing.

To toe the line as taught?

To make a spiral line skyward?

To draw a circle?

To feel what is wondrous about the quotes of great thinkers?

A glass of water. A ray of light upon thy brow. The Countenance of Forgiveness.

Magic Theatre

Down a certain alley way off an unlit street in an old borough of London there is a door with an inconspicuous awning that reads Magic Theatre. This theatre only conducts shows on equinoxes and solstices, its invitations are sent out a year prior; the list defined by esoteric accreditation; the house, on each of these propitious occasions, is packed. Tonights show consists of the transmogrification of a participatory audience by way of an alchemical recitation.

The man inside the coat roam sports a tuxedo. He takes raincoats, hats, umbrellas and isn't permitted to show any sign of facial expression. His name is Sebastian. Sebastian is exceedingly pleased to have acquired the work as it was a nepotistic job and quite difficult to come by. He recognized several of the attendees that evening, but like he was paid to do, was wont to show any indication of this recognition. The job paid exceedingly well and he resolved to keep it, regardless of certain occupational oddities.

Lady Madeline Levine passed her coat to this man whom she didn't notice. She quickly seized her date, Viscount Nicholas Coleridge's left arm, and whispered, "Let's get in and find our seats, I don't want to be late Nicholas." "Yes of course, dear." He softly replied. The lights in the house went dark. The curtains began an enchantingly slow withdrawal.

A few chairs squeaked, a muffled cough from the back row.

The spotlight appeared center stage on a man with a top hat, cane, bow-tie and a handle bar mustache. "Ladies and Gentleman, I need not inform you of the auspicious considerations behind this clandestine performance and thus remind you to remain seated and attentive throughout the entire show. "

The spotlight clips out. The room goes silent. The curtains draw shut once again and then re-open. From the back corner of the room a curious head peaks in to catch a glimpse of the action.

Sebastian had heard rumors of such plays but wished to see one for himself. Stage center a man dressed in a beaded blue robe knelt before another man, clad in all white, holding a white sword. A soft gasp ran through the crowd. Sebastian looked around to see if anybody noticed he'd poked his head in. The audience appeared rapt with attention, and unconcerned with his presence. Once knighted, the blue robed man rose, and turned to address the crowd.

"In the name of the great lineage, the holy beings and God beyond this world, in front of the planets, stars, moon and sun, I rise, anointed, by the almighty one."

A billow of smoke covered the stage and seeped out onto the audience. Sebastian felt the floor quiver beneath him. When he stepped back into the lobby, the ground became solid. He felt dizzy in his stomach and had a hard time looking at the walls. Sebastian quickly returned to his duties.

Whiling serving drinks during intermission, he was not allowed to accept gratuity. "Thank you, but we don't accept gratuity." He would say politely, while thinking, "Just who *are* these *people* whom I am serving?"

After the show Sebastian passed back raincoats, top hats, furs, gloves and canes to the guests. They retrieved their articles without noticing him. Had they known he'd seen? Was he safe? When the last of them departed Sebastian stepped out into the brisk London night and lit his tobacco pipe. He blew a plume of smoke upward and it drifted across the sign depicting the name of the theatre as it dimmed. Sebastian took a few more steps and looked back to find the door had become a wall, and the city a memory.

The Silence

Opening sentence worth its weight. Pitter patter, an elongated reference to the specific, a sign of mutual adoration, the descriptive picture of a natural setting. Obligatory voice injunction. Sensual yet sophisticated dialogue studying the positioning of an element. The part where it states it has something to say. The tantalizing end-goal towards which it is barreling. Reasons it may take a while to get there.

Shiny new development of context through setting. A jovial toned bodily description, "Something booming and practical," is spoken. "Some wititude which negates that." A lesser known word and a comma. The things we feel when unknown words are said to us.

Introspective narrative. Strident language in the tenor of effort and tenacity. A reference to

Greek mythology, particularly tragic. The part where you realize your author has an underbelly. A sudden burst of enjoying this now antiquated act of reading. Surprise.

Modest adoration of a cultural past time, e.g., baseball. A taste for its competitive nature and fascination with the mysticism of all games in general. Sudden explosion into a philosophy on the sound of a sunflower and its relation to a famous astronomer's Latin titled book. This little known fact (perhaps the key signature of the entire compilation), which was discovered in the penultimate copy of such and such by so and so.

Shrouded so as not to reveal too much. More elongated descriptions of that something specific, now poetically homonystic. The assertion that the author's characters either are or are not surrounded by a lot of books. Nothing in-between. A linguistic parable. The summary and point of it. The need to switch gears again, but cleverly.

At last a body of composition that demands transparency. Something about the sky inferring a metaphor for the life of a teething artist with a fierce overbite and little cathartic extrapolation.

The supposition that this narrator is in fact a have-lived type, perhaps even, an anti-hero; the listing of three quintessential anti-heroes (Don Quixote, Robin Hood, Lebowski). The affirmation of the capacity to speak about literature. The processing phenomenon that is consciousness realizing itself, and the discussion of this location on paper. A furthering of that ascending spiralic trajectory until the mechanism squeaks. The part where you may have lost some people. The part where you haven't lost others. Recollection of that attention span. Return to streamlined implication.

The need for window dressing. A bucolic way of affiliating with suburban locations. An affectation found in pop lyrics. Persistent pattern and voice.

Perfunctory admonition of too much information. The startling capacity to intrigue with *raw*-ness. Another more obvious attempt at taking that presupposition further than is really necessary or comfortable. A retreat from that framed by a foreknowing-ness that that furthering may return. Incisive character crisis conveniently occurs through internal dialogue.

Actual presupposition explicated in terms of salient motifs. Surreal distention of that application by way of reference to the indeterminate. The easiest line to digest. The joke. A bitter button. Self-aware mocking of bitterness. Mirth in self-awareness of bitterness. Satisfying but not altogether excellent landing. Last words that feel conclusivesque.

The Paradox of Mahmoud Al-Rahamid

The following suppositions were made by the Greatest Thinker in the World: words are not in fact separate, or discrete, as they seem to be nor are they ever strictly literal. Instead, they exist in a continuum of accumulating meaning. This is due to the constant ability to change the meaning of the previous word or words. For example, if I say, "I see you," the implication is that a person, namely, "you" are being "seen." And yet, if I add to this statement, "have disappeared," now an entirely different proposition exists. Further still, if I add "into your work," this now reverses the meaning again and infers the person *is* in fact there, but merely "not there" in the figurative sense that they are preoccupied with a particular task at hand and cannot be bothered.

What begins as seen then appears to be not seen, in the end means being seen in a removed manner. Here, in one sentence, comprise three different intents, each new word illustrating further clarity of the former. Because of this phenomenon (the capacity to repurpose the meaning of language that has previously been spoken), it is the the Greatest Thinker in the World's supposition that all speech is not composed of *discrete articulation*, but instead a string of *instances of inflection* that approach articulation (where articulation confers distinction from other sets of words). If true, then Language cannot carry *definite* meaning (though it *can* carry *temporal* and *figurative* meaning), because definite meaning, that is literal meaning would mean it would be immune to a redefinition of that meaning, but as we have just demonstrated, all language is subject to be redefined in the context of that which is about to follow it.

Thus, one wonders if humans will ever be able to articulate (make clear and distinct) what they mean at any given moment or maybe instead, can only inflect (color and reform) what they have said and in this manner clarify further what they want to mean with each successive element.

From this supposition the Greatest Thinker in the World surmised that the accretion of all speech, as a function of meaning, will never reach any singular definite meaning, but rather, is only approaching conclusivity, yet can never confirm it. As such, speech escapes meaning.

And yet to chose one word is to exclude another, there is death in speech. However, so long as this capacity to make more life exists (more words), and the vibration of sound the ability to satiate the human ear, then the notion that definite speech has been made will persist, ask publishers, or ministers, but in opposition to this, one might consider the supposition herein, (from the Greatest Thinker in the World) which is that this consideration is in fact a fallacy.

The author (whom is a far cry from one able to even allege such a supposition) believes, so long as our willingness to make sounds persists, meaning may remain yet entirely formed. Expression here is an infinite journey traversed only covering half the distance to the destination. The unreachability of this final "destination" *evokes* the holy and ineffable condition of Language (a *processes of aggregating sound* pockets that morph continually in accordance with greater and greater complex surroundings, enhancing signification in the *approach to signification* aimed toward some "point" where "words" suddenly "matter", that is, quite literally, *instantiate*. And at such point literal meanings would be possible.

Language, as constructed by Sound, is our primary vehicle for signification, though it may not be the mode by which we achieve it. Despite this, it *is* quite feasible that via evolving communications, the human species might better share not just sound pockets through speech, but more complex linguistic information which contains scent, tactility, and imagery.

Perhaps, in the future, when one says, "warm" another's temperature will increase and if you describe the sweet smell of butterscotch my nose will taste it. However, even with such enhanced developments as synesthesia, human Language would still be a ways off from complete signification itself, which is to say absolute meaning.

Consequently, words are like legos added onto previous legos of expression in an inexhaustible attempt to arrive at some sort of edifice (meaning via articulation) nuanced entirely by inflection (the coloring of the block) and within this overlapping (the connection between what is said and how it's meant) there is a necessary enveloping (just as a caterpillar wraps itself into a cocoon), and within this envelopment there is a necessary redefining (the dissolution of the contents within that construct), and from this a necessary jump between what one usually says (as a propulsion of what one desires to mean) and what one wants to say, (from an objective consideration of what has expressed by what one said) until ultimately, an articulation has been achieved (this reappears in a metamorphic state).

The Greatest Thinker in the World inserted a point of fact here (if facts can be asserted in a *literal* sense, because facts, in their traditional sense do not exist as real but merely plausible in relation to what is perceived as factual in the current context of the progression of human gnosis, which itself is continually folding outward from and into upon itself, reformulating its own body, from what has been considered "known" and "true" - e.g., we come from fish, there is no God, there is nothing smaller than the atom, into what may also be true, we were painted by an artist, we are not alone but rather held, the world is infinitely small and vast, and that what is "more than us-ness" is also within us-ness, and everything else is as well, such that what were once "truths" reveal themselves to be theories, and not *laws*, e.g., gravity is a theory and not a *law*, secretly it is a belief held stubbornly, a little known fact is that the most accurate beliefs don't come from theories, they come from a fount of inner-knowingness, they come with an internal alignment with the flow of growth, the observation of experience, and the bitter embrace of wisdom), is that if everything ever spoken got wrapped up into one big strand of words and strung itself in circumnavigation around our planet, and then wove its way out from there ascending like a linguistic Tower of Babel up into our star system and the heavens above, and if this spiral staircase were to become a single monadic implication amidst all the participatory elements contained in that journey, all the legos, every color, then, at that point, — much like the paradox developed by the 14th century thinker Mahmoud Al-Rahamid, (who asked if one could possibly taste their own tongue), — all of humanity would have the benefit of figuring out just exactly what it means to say.

Bill and His Ball

Bill suspected the earth was round. He was nearly certain of it. More than a year of research had led him to this conclusion. Unfortunately for Bill, he was up against more than five centuries of well oiled industrial-scientific disinformation, which assured him the earth was not round, but was instead, flat like a pancake.

"Flat like a pancake?" Bill said, That's crazy!"

But the scientists said that *he* was crazy because it was *indeed* flat like a pancake, perhaps flat like a *blueberry* pancake where the crests of the blueberries were the tips of the mountains, and the valley's were places where, for metaphor's sake, excited children had finger-picked some of the fruit out in advance to create divots before applying the syrup.

Bill wouldn't have any of it, he knew they had private interests in their flat earth geocentric corruption, the kind bent on making a God game out of a known accident. Bill spoke out,

"We're on a ball. You can tell it's a ball because ships going out to sea disappear over the curve of the earth."

"But Bill, the scientist's said, those ships aren't actually disappearing over the horizon they're simply traveling beyond one's visual line of sight. If you grab a pair of binoculars or a high-powered camera and rack focus on the place they disappeared from, those same ships pop right back into view. They're not heading 'over the horizon', they're just passing beyond the vanishing point of your perspective. Go see for yourself. Plus horizon comes from horizontal, meaning level."

These scientists and their word games, he thought. Bill retorted with all his might.

"Actually, we're on a ball tilted at 23.5 degrees that spins at 1,000 mph while traveling at a velocity of 67,000 mph around the sun and that sun — and all the planets along with it — rotates around the center of our Milky Way galaxy at

500,000 mph. Meanwhile, the *milky way galaxy* itself moves nearly three times faster than that, heading extragalactically at a speed of 1.3 million mph towards the constellation Lyra."

The scientists laughed. They said, "Woah, woah, slow dow, Bill. That's a lot of numbers! Let's break them down one by one. For starters, does the earth feel titled? If so, why isn't one of your legs muscularly larger to compensate for all the extra-work?"

"Well that's just absurd."

"More absurd than there is a tilt with no indication of a tilt? Okay, if the earth is spinning at 1,000 mph *and* orbiting at 67,000 mph, and traveling at 500,000 mph then how come, on a windless day I can watch a leaf rock back and forth toward the ground, without the slightest indication of any counter forces being present, such as tilt, spin or orbital speed?

"Easy. We're *in* our atmosphere, which moves along with it."

"We're *in* our atmosphere? Sounds like a Zoolander quote, 'The files are *in*side the computer?'"

"We're in it."

"So if I jump up in the air, this atmosphere carries me at 1,000 mph?

"That's right."

"Impressive, must be sticky. And what happens to all the people on the bottom of your ball earth? Don't they fall off?

"Nope, Gravity holds them in place."

"It holds cities upside down? You're telling me Buenos Aires is held upside down?

"Yep, and Sydney, and Johannesburg..."

"So let me get this right, if I jump, mm kay, and this sticky atmosphere catches me in the air and carries me at 1,000 mph while an invisible force called gravity holds me upside down all without my noticing it?"

"That's right."

"But what about the Coriolis effect? Are planes not subject to the same laws of physics as bullets? When you fly on a plane, why does the earth not spin beneath it?

"The atmosphere rotates with the earth proportionally faster the greater the height."

"But if the earth and its atmosphere spins west-east at about 1,000 mph at the equator, and planes fly at 10,000 feet through this spinning atmosphere at, conservatively, say 500 mph, then flights flying east-west into the spin should arrive at their destinations three times faster and flights flying west east in the same direction as the spin would go backwards."

"It does take about an hour longer to fly from NY to SF than SF to NY. It's the jet stream."

"If i'm flying to San Francisco around 500 mph, and the earth and the atmosphere is spinning towards me in the plane at over 1,000 mph, that means, San Francisco is approaching two times faster than the plane I'm in heading towards it. It's like I'm moving 1,500 mph from NY to SF, but going the other way, at 500 mph, with the earth spinning beneath me at 1,000 mph, should mean the plane will be going 500 mph in reverse, and end up somewhere in the middle of the Pacific ocean!"

"It's difficult to explain. The atmosphere moves along with the plane."

"You're a tough nut to crack Bill. Let us try a different line of questioning. If the sun is 90 million miles away, then how come it looks like it's the exact same size as the moon, which you say is vastly closer?"

"That's an optical effect. The moon is 400 times *nearer* to us than the sun. And the Sun is 400 times *larger* than the moon. They just *appear* the same size."

"Woah, woah, woah, hold the ponies. An optical effect? You mean to tell us, Bill, and bear with us here because we're the scientists who study all celestial phenomena with our big expensive telescopes, and don't believe in coincidence, that you think the sun *just so happens* to be exactly 400 times the size of the moon, and also the moon, *just so happens* to be exactly 400 times closer to the earth than the sun?"

"That's right."

"Occam's razor, Bill. What's more likely? The sun and the moon are the same size, in actual celestial balance of day and night, just as they appear to be, or one just so happens to be 400 times farther from us while the other just happens to be 400 times smaller, creating a cosmic coincidental fraction of perceptual equivalence?"

"Perhaps Occam cut himself while shaving."

"To what degree of improbability do you except us to stomach!? *You're* always going on about coincidences. We're scientists, and we find such a coincidence to be preposterously unlikely!

"It is an elusive matter of proportions."

"Elusive proportions, eh? Well, may we ask you this. If the earth travels 300 million miles between equinoxes from one spot on one side of the sun to the other, then why do all stars in the north remain in perfect orbit around Polaris? Wouldn't that vast distance cause some parallax, that is, a displacement of those perfect concentric rings around the north star?

"Polaris is *super* far away."

"Ah right.. How far away is super far away?"

"About 2,058,000,000 miles away."

"Okay one, we're not even sure that's a number. Two, now you're telling us what seems to not be moving, our earth, is in fact traveling at 70,000 mph rip-roaring through the galaxy, covering a tremendous distance of 300 million miles in a mere six months, but we can't measure a shift in the stars of a single inch?"

Bill fidgeted in his chair, and stammered ever so faintly, at the onset of his next point,

"It's all.. it's all just *too far away* to tell. Polaris is over four quadrillion miles away, three hundred million miles doesn't even register. Appearances can be deceiving. The sun. The moon. The stars. Just goes to show you can't trust your senses'!"

"Interesting line of reason, Bill. We can't trust our senses? The same senses that tell you to jump out of the way of an oncoming car? That enable a center fielder to predict the position of a baseball hit from 350 feet away while running at a full sprint solely from hearing the sound it made as it ricocheted off the bat? We've got news for you. Our senses are pretty gosh darn accurate."

Bill believed the earth was a ball and wasn't fooled by such logical approaches; he didn't care if any one else trusted him.

"It's a ball!" Bill said.

"Bill, sadly to say, if everybody thought the earth was a ball, and that we rotated around the sun, then we wouldn't be the center of a mysterious creation in a unique realm. Instead, we'd be a spec of dust floating in a cosmic accident that blindly thrashed its way from fire to Mozart. Does that really sound like a world you want to live in?"

"My world is no less divine for believing we live on a ball."

"Granted, and we hope you enjoy it! But pray it does not snatch your faith away from you. For that is a dangerously unscientific world where Tesla, Goethe, Tyco Brahe and Rudolf Steiner were all wrong."

"It's a ball." Bill stated, and no amount of scientific evidence could persuade him otherwise.

Ice Water

A mired sense of sunset cuts in from above two saloon-styled swinging doors. Backs line the bar in anonymity. A sole fly buzzes about nearly matching the soft electronic fuzz from the neon beer sign mounted in the window. The sign's halogenic glare blots out any natural impression of that sunset. The ventilation in this establishment is unkind to asthmatics. It is chewy, fermented, filled with melancholy.

A grandfather clock in the corner of the tavern, since stopped, is covered with dust. One patron, (who knows when), ventured to finger-pencil a word onto the clock's right twice-a-day face.

The bartender wears a placid expression, and cleans a mug with a rag. A man sporting a trucker's hat which says, ALL STEEL, INC, slams his soda can onto the counter. A different wiry lad with a tattered work coat and a somber configuration lifts a finger, a plea for more drink. The room smells of implacability and desultory hygiene. The bartender sees the finger, and walks over.

"What'll it be?"

"Pepsi Max."

"Comin' right up."

The bartender waves his hand over a silver sheet, causing it to glide leftward, reaches inside and withdraws a plastic 20 oz bottle of Pepsi Max. The wiry lad says "Thanks," and places his hand on a mouse-pad-sized mount on the counter, a beep sounds and the bartender nods approval. The man to the right of the one who'd just ordered finishes the remainder of his Diet Coke, and emits a burp worthy of the title, "the flatulent man's trumpet"; this man grumbles and snorts simultaneously at his indulgence. The trumpeter looks half-way in the direction of the wiry lad, "Aspartame makes me burp." The wiry man with his hand around the Pepsi Max responds, "Creates neurological disorders too, but guys like us can't afford anything else." The trumpeter lifts his soda, "Yeeeuup." A waft of commiseration sprouts along the bar. A poindexter-looking guy seated at a table in the back takes a sip of Tab. He sits beside his date, a red head covered in freckles with wide frame glasses who drinks Coca-Cola Zero and says little. He draws spirals along the top half of her back meditatively between sips.

The saloon style swinging doors at the entrance push open with an unprecedented intimacy. The kind that creates a sharp incongruous squeak throughout the room and draws a half-dozen necks in tandem. The neon sign buzzes extra loudly and clips out, leaving only the fly's noise to continue the drone. The bartender catches himself staring and polishes a soda can just after to appear composed. She dresses in leather made from pineapple and sports green spectacles. Her blond hair falls behind her shoulder blades agreeably. The deer-in-headlights effect in the room isn't new to her; she treats it indifferently, thereby enhancing it. By the time she sits down two men have subtly leaned closer and the bartender has his chest to the bar.

"What can I get you ma'am?"

"Water."

"Wah wah, *water*?"

"Yes. *Water*."

The man in the back with the Tab and his date both take in a short breath implying surprise. The woman with the matching white purse adjusts her seat on the stool. The bartender grapples with the delivery.

"Dah dah dah, dah ya want ice?"

"Yes."

"Cubes are more than thirty..."

"I know."

"Ah ha, hah, how-how many cubes, mam?"

"Two."

"*Twoooo* cubes?'

"Yes."

"Do you know how mah mah much I have to charge for..."

The woman snaps again, "Yes."

"Oh-kay! Coming right up ma'am."

The bartender lifts a heavy ring of keys and sorts through them for a tiny brass plated square shaped one; he puts it into a cube safe-looking object to the left of the brass-plated refrigerator. Upon turning the key a blue light pierces upward from a deep cool freezer. The bartender adorns a pair of white gloves, and picks up the chilled metal tongs affixed to its interior edge, and begins to remove two cubes of ice.

The barflies lean over to catch a glimpse. The blue light beams upward upon the bartender's face like the sky looking down. One by one, he places them in her cup, and then places the cup under a key-locked spout, which he turns on from a different key on his ring, filling the glass with cool, fresh and clean spring water. The bartender sets the drink in front of her. It appears strange in the room, like an explorer in Antarctica, or a man standing on the moon.

"Ha.. ha.. here ya' go ma ma'am."

"Thank you," she says and with great deftness and a gentility places her palm on the mouse-pad sized mount.

That finger-penciled word upon the face of the dusty since-stopped Grandfather clock in the back reads, "THIRST".

Tabacita

A concatenation of neorealism, cultural dyslexia,
and a-rhythmic humor, Alonso Clemente's
Tabacita, which takes place ten years hence, is an
Indy Mexican Dramedy set in Los Angeles. One
half of its hero, Gabriel (José Alvarez), spelunks
about East LA with his paternal twin, Martina
(Maria Garcia), chirping Linklater-esque dialogue
in fluent Spanish on what it means to be American
(English is only an operational-defunct setting
spawned by the characters' disillusionment with
the medium for most of act one), all amidst the
crumbling and jarring architecture of East LA,
seen through a smoggy lens as a kind of
hackneyed devalued character.

The movie is a sort of *politico-defacto*, both with
its racially-charged subplot - Martina is in the US
illegally - and the fact that the dynamic duo are

budding coders for a group called the RIC, "Radical Information Collective" (Think EFF-type but hackers). By modeling a program after their twin-speak language the wiry pair invent a novel form of stacking information that affords them an internship with a recalcitrant software developer Greg (Wayne Cordoski) in the now bourgeois *Silicon Beach* (Venice Beach, Director Clemente's hometown) for an unnamed corporate conglomerate (ahem, Google, anyone?).

Thrown between the prospect of money and principles, the Twins, one part captivated one part disillusioned with this "Traje" ("Suit"), as they call him, and his world of Corporicana, vacillate over wether or not to stay. Wayne Cordoski's portrayal of Greg, as a sort of *Finding Forrester* meets *Boiler Room* mentor, is distinct, if not redeemable. The pair's time at the company offers, if possible, a nuanced look at an Orwellian metaphor.

Ultimately, Gabriel continues the apprenticeship with Greg and Martina returns to East LA and the RIC. The telepathic component of the program they created heightens as their paths dovetail, forcing a poetic reconciliation of oppositional motifs.

Hacktivist coding scenes pumped with a sort of visual-Ritalin editing style gilded by what sounds like pseudo-psychedelic *Tool* covers are successful, but the techy side of the film ultimately steers away from this "matrixy" attitude, veering instead towards a primarily mundane, if not raw, depiction of young talent discovering their craft (think *Portrait of an Artist* meets *Madame Bovary*).

Castor H. Dominguez's screenplay places complex characters between the simulacra of corporate reality and what feels like an iron curtain of cultural immigration. Questions on the nature of security, and freedom pepper an up-beat ride through these digitized frameworks. José Alvarez's depiction of Gabriel transitions from an intellectually taught assault upon the faceless wall of capitalism into an interest in information platforms and access to understanding them.

The final turnkey for the film is that the company Gabriel thought he understood blackmails him to disclose the whereabouts of the RIC. Gabriel must decide between giving up the anarchist group and therefore his sister, or facing imprisonment and flushing the promising future that is being offered to him. The moment of truth will not disappoint. Overall, *Tabacita* or "Little Tobacco", simplifies where convolution looms, and charms where formula once reigned.

"Tabacita" is rated R (Under 17 requires accompanying parent or adult guardian) for strong language, brief sexual content and situational mundanity. In Spanish, with English subtitles. Running time: 1: hour 39 minutes.

The Professor's Assistant

That someone should endeavor to write a volume such as, *'The History of Counter-Culture from Punk Rock to Ai Wei-Wei'*, was beyond Petra, the post-graduate research assistant whom was hired by the eccentric (perhaps, one must admit, this adjective is redundant) Lit-Theory Professor at Nubes University, to scour its every line and letter in search of a reference to what he'd called, "a mystagogue-ical *je ne sies quoi*". When Petra had attempted to seek further clarification the Professor exclaimed, "Don't speak student! For fear that you should insult the *mysterium tremendum* with a categorical impudence!" He then rushed out of the room *as if* having become suddenly aware of a pressing appointment.

Petra had been awarded this assistantship to the illustrious and semi-infamous Professor, after winning a university wide essay contest, limited to 1,001 words, on why books mattered. She'd determined therein, and perhaps heretically so, that "book" as a word to describe writing, once typically compiled onto paper, and consisting of topics either fictional or non-fictional, and of varying lengths, was in itself, anachronistic. She proposed instead an alternate name for books, and then went on to defend her reasoning at length, to some success.

Petra wrote, "For the *book* itself, comes from the Old English *Boc*, meaning a written document or charter, and before that the Germanic *Bocian*, meaning to grant by charter, while it only bares passing semblance to the English *Beech*, a tree from which Runes were carved[2]."

Petra argued and the English department at Nubes University at least democratically agreed, that "books", and novels specifically as having reached the tallest imaginary heights of man,

---

[2] Runes were considered a 'divining' tool, and thus to make them, a divine act in and of itself. It is mythologized that the first stones were cast by the mere pronunciation of the word which became a symbol inscribed upon it.

would better be termed "charters", for authors are like sovereign creative powers, whom grant specific rights (such as the right to imagine, the right to hold dear, or the right to speculate), to its readers (which constitute groups, like brands or schools - even possibly the school referred to herein, or metropoles).

Petra asserted that this *inherent contract* was the only thing present in *every* book, and thus was far more intrinsic with respect to the *raison d'etre* of literature, than a vestigial reference to having once been printed on dead trees, (though charter is from Latin *Chartula* meaning, "little paper.") She claimed, "The Great American Charter" will one day replace "The Great American Novel". This new *signifier* (as Derrida lovingly referred to them), she continued, "was a superior choice for the *signified* in question, because it inferred the sovereign power of an author's imagination, and the agreement with its readers whom pay it attention." She went on at length about how the right to participate in an author's imagination is like being hired, or *chartered*, and then added, "In the modern age, as we are less-and-less tethered to he physicality of matter, why not use a signifier hat remains bound to the spirit of its signified? Novels will always be charters between readers nd writers."

From there, Petra restated her thesis in the nal paragraph of that essay, that *books are charters because they hire the reader to pay attention*, and that ovels are stored in the minds of readers primarily, nd in print secondarily. This last contention ontained a flourish, which no doubt, heavily nfluenced the final decision on her essay. "The atin word for Library, *librum* literally means, 'the nner bark of trees', but our Libraries are not kept n trees. They are stored in the hearts of readers. Can we not change - even today - the meaning of words to better depict our reality?"

Whilst perusing chapter three subsection our's seventh footnote Petra looked toward the oor near the back of the empty auditorium. From where she sat in the place The Professor typically rated from - albeit often with one shoe lace ntied or the buttons along his front shirt off-kilter but in a room now occupied only by the certainty f silence, it seemed to her, that she may have ound something of what he'd been alluding to.

www.ingramcontent.com/pod-product-compliance
Lightning Source LLC
Chambersburg PA
CBHW051841020726
47502CB00005B/1903